LAUGHTER LINES

DAVID MBOWA RUBADIRI

SWEETSPIRE LITERATURE
MANAGEMENT

LAUGHTER LINES

1. Why is perfume expensive?
    You pay per fume.

2. Why are Graduates unmarried?

    They have a bachelor's degree.

3. Couples are most excited during the week of passion.

4. Why are people at the well great artists?

    They draw water.

5.   Why do rivers have business acumen?

They own banks.

6.   Which holes are unexciting?

Boring holes.

7. Why are women not perfectly happy about the man they marry on their wedding day?

   Its not the best man they marry.

8. Which people are partially single, partially married?

   Midwives.

9.   Boy: Interesting, in just one day I will be an adult.

Auntie: Really?

Boy: Yeah, in our school assembly today, our headmaster told us to get ready for tomorrow since the children of today are the adults of tomorrow.

10. Boy: My brother has what it takes to be an athlete.

    Trainer: Are you sure?

    Boy: Very sure, even his doctor would back me on this, the other day I heard him tell him 'I know it is hard to believe this but you have athletes foot.'

11. Girl: I am no longer going to use the highway

Mum: Why?

Girl: I am joining the assertive girls club this week and according to the head girl one of the things we are required to do before we enrol is to abandon our old ways.

12. Why does Jim have legs on his nose?

His nose is always running.

13. Did you see the spy who loved me?

No, but I have watched the film.

14. When do lawyers become tailors?

    When they are working on a suit.

15. While in golf the goal is to put the balls in that hole, in sakes the goal is to keep the balls outside that hole.

16. When do cars cry?

    When they break down.

17. Man: Is your dad an optician?

Boy: No, why?

Man: Someone told me he and his team are working on new eyes.

Boy: Oh, no, thats the Mercedes new eyes.

18. Dad, why do they have to call heads of state presidents?

Because they are the ones that the press dents.

19. Why do you keep denying you are a doubting Thomas?

Because my name is not Thomas.

20. When does a house go missing?

When its owners move house.

21. My parents moved house.

My, they must have very strong muscles.

22. Which Jam is unappetising?

   Traffic Jam.

23. Did you pass with flying colours?

   No only I and Richard passed and by the way who is flying colours, I know no one who goes by that name.

24. Why don't you go for mass on Christmas?

   It is Chris's mass not mine.

25. Your son is going down in history.

Wrong, he is going up in his story.

26. Why are you so lean and tall?

My teacher said you look what you eat so I started eating spaghetti.

27. Man: Is the assembly going to be held in August?

    Boy: Why?

    Man: They said it's going to be an august assembly.

28. Man: Have you seen the Vicar?

    Boys: You mean they have made a car by that name?

29. Why do you say your dad is underemployed?

He works in a submarine.

30. Why is all the mice on the run?

Hell broke loose, it rained dogs and cats.

31. Why do trousers have insects?

   They have flys.

32. When does the door ask you a question?

   When you answer it.

33. Has she been amputated?

   Why?

   Someone on TV was told she has her legs.

34. Why does the town have hair?

   The police is combing it.

35. Which Roman emperor has something to do
   with hair?

   Ceaser.

36. Why are rivers rich?

   They have banks.

37. Why does the singer lack a heart?

    He sang his heart out on his recent show.

38. Bankers have crude minds-they usually ask:

    Are you depositing or withdrawing?

39. What do buses and bicycles have in common?

    They are ridden.

40. A newspaper error read:

Minister raped woman for criticizing govt. It should have read-Minister rapped woman for criticizing govt.

41. When do people become artists?

When they draw money.

42. What is interesting about the gap between the male sex and the female sex?

It is a productive one.

43. How many Shakespaere plays have you read?

2.

Which ones?

Romeo and Juliet.

44. The battle between the sexes is certainly a productive one. I mean its the reason we are here.

45. What is the sweetest cream?

Icecream.

46. Sports teams need alcohol to win games. Why?

    Its team spirit that enables them to win games.

47. What is the coldest cream?

    Icecream.

48. Which cream is eaten?

Icecream.

49. Did you sing with feeling?

No, i sang with Patrick.

50. A bookshop is where books hope.

51. Child: Mum, why does auntie think I am sick- she keeps saying she is going to give me a treat tomorrow.

52. Postpone the election for nine months since thats when all the women will be in labour.

53. When are rivers amazed?

When they wander.

54. Newspaper error-Tongue in chic (should have read-tongue in cheek).

55. When do you apply cosmetics to your mind?

When you make up your mind.

56. What is the funniest card in a pack of cards?

The joker.

57. Why do you say the coming elections are the fourth?

They keep referring to them as the fourth coming elections.

58. What does Mathematics and Politics have in common?

Rulers.

59. When is a meeting in your hands?

When it is held.

60. What do cars and cows have in common?

Horns.

61. When do you have 3 eyes?

When someone keeps an eye on you.

62. Which people have a sense of lying?

People with a licence.

63. Why are you spraying the animals with water?

I was asked to water them.

64. Why do you say he is an artist?

They said as he talked he drew a crowd of listeners.

65. Why do you say lawyers like alcohol?

They have a bar.

66. Which is the sweetest comb?

The honeycomb.

67. What kind of course do couples do to get deeper knowledge of each other?

Inter-course.

68. Why is hair naked?

   It needs a hairdresser.

69. Which stock has human qualities?

   A laughing stock.

70. What happens during the battle of the sexes?

   The men and women keep changing positions.

71. Which stock is funny?

   Laughing stock.

72. Why does making kids take a bit of drilling?

   It is always said she bore him a son.

73. Which sticks have feet?

   Walking sticks.

74. Why do VIPS need bicycles?

They usually have spokesmen.

75. Most male tennis fans pay attention during the serve-that is when the doubles can be caught with their pants down.

76. When do laws become vegetables?

When you repeal them.

77. The battle of the sexes is about positioning-i mean all that people talk about is the men being on top.

78. Man: That is an ice cream.

Boy: What part of the face do you apply it to?

Man: The mouth.